Pictures Presents

W9-BWY-668

THE PRINCE AND THE PAUPER

Adapted by Fran Manushkin
Illustrated by Russell Schroeder and Don Williams

A GOLDEN BOOK • NEW YORK
Western Publishing Company, Inc., Racine, Wisconsin 53404

MCMXCIII

Once upon a time there was a good and kindly king. He ruled his country with fairness and generosity.

But one day the king became very ill and could no longer watch over his kingdom. His son, the prince, worried by his father's bedside.

"Aha," said the greedy captain of the guards. "Now my friends and I can steal from all the king's subjects!" And day after day they filled up the palace with mountains of food and trunks of gold.

It seemed that nobody could save the kingdom from the thieving captain. Then one day...

... two peasants hoping to find something to eat wandered near the palace.

It just happened that one of the paupers, Mickey, looked exactly like the king's son, the prince. But this beggar boy's life was not like the life of the prince. Mickey had no fine clothes to wear nor a fancy palace to live in. But he *did* have two loyal friends. One was a bumbling fellow named Goofy, and the other was a large, friendly dog named Pluto.

Mickey and Goofy watched as the captain of the guards sped by in the royal coach. "Look at those delicious turkey drumsticks," sighed Mickey.

"Woof, woof," barked the hungry Pluto as he chased the coach toward the palace.

"Stop!" shouted Mickey. "Come back!" He dashed away after the dog.

Pluto chased the royal coach to the gates of the
palace, with Mickey right behind him. To Mickey's
surprise, the royal guard waved him in—and called
him "Your Majesty."

"Our prince is certainly dressed oddly today,"
thought the guard. "And he's got himself a new dog,
too."

By now, Goofy had lost sight of Mickey and
wondered where he'd disappeared to.

Meanwhile, inside the palace, the real prince was sitting through a boring lesson. To amuse himself, he took out his peashooter and aimed it at his servant, Donald.

"Wak!" shouted Donald when he got hit. He shot a pea back at the prince. But he missed the prince and hit the tutor, who tossed him out of the room.

At that moment, all of them heard a loud crash near the palace entrance. They ran to see what the noise was and saw a suit of armor rolling around on the floor.

"I'm sorry," said a voice inside the armor. "I guess I got tangled up."

Then the prince saw a face peering out of the helmet—a face that looked exactly like his!

Both the prince and the pauper screamed.

After Mickey explained who he was, the prince took him into his room so they could have a talk.

"Oh," sighed the prince, "how happy your life must be. You never have to take any boring lessons and you can wander and play all day."

"But you go to feasts all the time," said Mickey, whose empty stomach was growling.

"I have a wonderful idea," said the prince. "Why don't you and I change places for a day?"

Mickey hesitated. "I don't think that would work at all. I don't know how to be a prince."

"Oh, it's easy," the prince assured him. And soon Mickey and the prince had exchanged clothes.

Then the prince gaily waved good-bye and dashed out the door of the palace. This time, the captain of the guards, seeing a boy who looked like a peasant, angrily booted him and his dog over the wall and into a snowbank.

"Ha," the prince chuckled. "My disguise is working. My own guard didn't recognize me!"

But the prince didn't fool Pluto. A quick sniff and a closer look told the dog this boy was *not* his old friend. Pluto sadly walked away.

"Hey, there you are!" shouted Goofy. "I've been looking all over for you!"

"Uh, hello!" said the prince. He did not know the pauper's friend and quickly rushed away.

    Back at the palace, Donald brought food to
Mickey's room. Mickey, very hungry, reached for it,
but Donald snatched it away. "I'm checking for
poison," he said, biting into a turkey leg and
smacking his lips.

    The smell of food was driving Mickey crazy, and he
was afraid Donald would eat his entire lunch.
"Thanks," said Mickey, grabbing the leg back from
Donald. Then he pushed the duck out the door and
slammed it behind him.

"Now it's time for your falconry lesson," said the tutor, showing Mickey how to control the bird. But instead of making the *falcon* fly, the angry bird chased Mickey and made *him* fly—in the opposite direction!

The horseback-riding lesson didn't go any better— Mickey kept falling off the horse!

Meanwhile, the real prince had decided to try
sledding through the snow with the peasants.
Unfortunately, he tripped and tumbled down the hill,
becoming a giant snowball!

The prince rolled and rolled and rolled down to a
busy marketplace. And there, to his astonishment, the
prince saw the captain of the guards stealing food
from the peasants!

"Stop!" ordered the prince, but the guards didn't
recognize him and kept on stealing. "I had no idea our
guards were taking food from the people," said the
prince. "There'll certainly be some changes when I get
back to the palace."

Just then a royal food wagon appeared. "Give these
people food," the prince ordered the guard, showing
him his royal ring.

"Yes, sir," said the guard when he saw the ring. But
the cruel captain and his men came dashing through
the crowd, trying to steal the food right back. They
shoved the people, and the prince as well. Luckily,
Goofy came along and helped him to escape.

"You saved my life!" the prince said gratefully.

Just a few minutes later the town crier came by and announced that the good king had died.

"I must go to the palace right away," said the prince. "I will miss my father greatly, but now it is my duty to take over as king."

"Gosh," said Goofy. "You're the prince. I didn't know. I thought you were my old buddy Mickey."

"I am your friend from now on," vowed the prince as he rushed away toward the palace.

At the palace, the prince was greeted by the captain of the guards. "I see your royal ring," the captain said. "But it won't do you any good." He grabbed the prince and tossed him into the dungeon. "As soon as the pauper is crowned king," said the captain, "I shall unmask him as an impostor and rule the kingdom myself!"

The prince soon discovered that he had company. Donald was in the dungeon, too.

The prince stared at the locked door. "If I don't get
out in time for my coronation, our kingdom will be
ruined!"

Just then the door down the hall opened and a
prison guard rushed in. He was a very strange guard
who stumbled and bumped into everyone. He
bumped hardest against the other guard, who tumbled
right down to the floor.

"Hi, prince," the guard giggled. It wasn't a guard at all. It was Goofy!

"You saved my life again," said the prince. Then the prince took the keys and unlocked the dungeon, and everybody dashed out.

Meanwhile, in the throne room, Mickey was trying desperately to wriggle away from the royal crown. "Please don't put it on my head," he begged.

"He is not the prince!" yelled the evil captain. "He's an impostor! Seize him!"

"But *I'm* not an impostor!" came a voice from the balcony. It was the real prince!

The prince was crowned king, and his first act was to arrest the evil captain and all his scheming friends.

Everybody in the kingdom was happy again—especially Pluto, who was reunited with his old friend Mickey.

From that day on, the new king, like his father, ruled with kindness and generosity. He always remembered his day as a pauper, and he saw to it that nobody went hungry.

He made Goofy captain of the guards, and Mickey became the provider of food.

Together they created a wonderful kingdom for all!